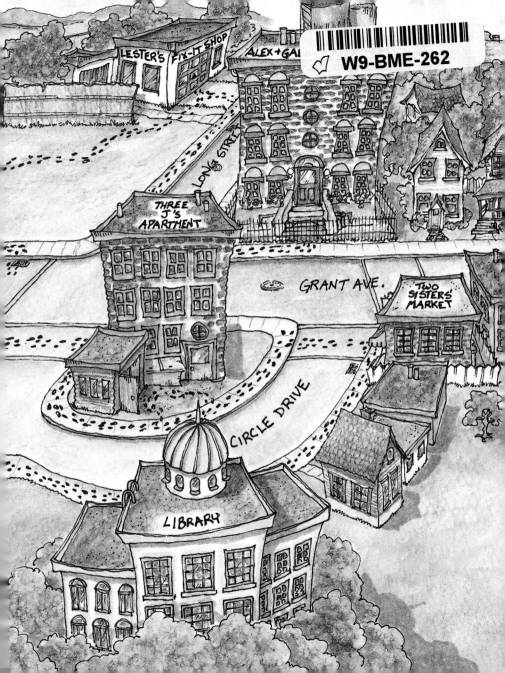

Rookie
choices®

THE SPARKLE THING

Written by Larry Dane Brimner • Illustrated by Christine Tripp

Children's Press®
A Division of Scholastic Inc.
New York • Toronto • London • Auckland • Sydn
Mexico City • New Delhi • Hong Kong
Danbury, Connecticut

For Doug and Jackie
—L.D.B.

For my grandson Brandon
—C.T.

Reading Consultants

Linda Cornwell

Coordinator of School Quality and Professional Improvement
(Indiana State Teachers Association)

Katharine A. Kane

Education Consultant

(Retired, San Diego County Office of Education and San Diego State University)

Library of Congress Cataloging-in-Publication Data

Brimner, Larry Dane.
    The sparkle thing / by Larry Dane Brimner; illustrated by Christine Tripp.
        p. cm. — (Rookie choices)
    Summary: Gabby takes a pretty sparkle thing from the market without paying for it and must face the consequences.
    ISBN 0-516-22159-0 (lib. bdg.)   0-516-25978-4 (pbk.)
    [1. Stealing—Fiction.] I. Tripp, Christine, ill. II. Title. III. Series.
PZ7.B767 Sp 2001
[E]—dc21   00-047566

This book is about **honesty**.

Gabby couldn't take her eyes off the sparkle thing. It made tiny rainbows fall on the floor and walls.

"Gabriela, please,"
her grandmother said.

"Sorry, Abuela," Gabby said. She had almost forgotten she was in Two Sisters' Market.

Gabby followed along after her grandmother. But she stopped to look again at the sparkle thing and the rainbows it made.

9

Later that day, the Corner Kids
met at Gabby's. That's what
Gabby, Alex, and Three J called
themselves. Gabby showed her
friends the sparkle thing.

11

"Cool!" said Three J.

"Where did you get it?" asked Alex.

The question made Gabby feel funny, but just then her grandmother walked in.

Gabby slipped the sparkle thing into her pocket without answering.

15

"Anyone for chocolate cake?" Gabby's grandmother asked.

"Yes, please," said Three J.

"Yum," said Alex.

"Gabriela, why don't you help me carry the plates?"

17

"Can we look at the
sparkle thing again?"
asked Three J.

"What sparkle thing?"
Gabby's grandmother asked.

19

Gabby slowly pulled the sparkle thing from her pocket. She looked at the rainbows on the floor. They did not look as beautiful now as they had before.

"I took it from the market," Gabby said quietly.

"You took it without paying?" her grandmother asked.

Gabby nodded.
"I'm sorry, Abuela," she said.

23

"You do not owe *me* the apology," her grandmother said.

Gabby bit her lip, and tears filled her eyes. She knew her grandmother was right.

Three J and Alex didn't say a word as Gabby left.

At the market, Gabby went to the tall sister. "I took this without paying," she said. It was the hardest thing she ever had to say. "I'm sorry."

27

The tall sister held the sparkle thing in the air. "Everyone missed this," she said.

Then she hung it back in the window. "Now our rainbows will bring smiles to their faces again."

29

Just then, a rainbow fell on
the floor, and the tall sister smiled.

Gabby smiled, too. She knew the
sparkle thing was where it belonged.

31

ABOUT THE AUTHOR

Larry Dane Brimner studied literature and writing at San Diego State University and taught school for twenty years. The author of more than seventy-five books for children, many of them Children's Press titles, he enjoys meeting young readers and writers when he isn't at his computer.

ABOUT THE ILLUSTRATOR

Christine Tripp lives in Ottawa, Canada, with her husband Don; four grown children—Elizabeth, Erin, Emily, and Eric; son-in-law Jason; grandsons Brandon and Kobe; four cats; and one very large, scruffy puppy named Jake.

SPINNINGWHEEL
BIKE
SHOP

COTTONWOOD SCHOOL

COTTONWOOD STREET

LONG STREET